CAPTAIN BEASTLIE'S Pirate Party

For all my piratical nephews and great-nephews,
old and young, with a great big grubalicious
"YO HO HO!" L.C.

First published in 2014 by Nosy Crow Ltd
The Crow's Nest, 10a Lant Street
London SE1 1QR
www.nosycrow.com

ISBN 978 0 85763 111 4 (HB)
ISBN 978 0 85763 112 1 (PB)

Nosy Crow and associated logos are trademarks and/or registered
trademarks of Nosy Crow Ltd.

A CIP catalogue record for this book is available from the British Library.

Printed in China
Papers used by Nosy Crow are made from wood
grown in sustainable forests.

3 5 7 9 8 6 4 2 (HB)
5 7 9 8 6 4 (PB)

CAPTAIN BEASTLIE'S Pirate Party

nosy crow

Lucy Coats   Chris Mould

Captain Beastlie
was the grubbiest and smelliest
pirate to sail the
Seven Salty Seas.

But . . .

... Captain Beastlie's ship was smart and his crew were squeaky-clean.

One grey and grimsome Monday, Captain Beastlie rolled out of bed. Five rotten cabbages rolled out, too. "Only **5 days** left till m'birthday!" he roared, picking a bogey out of his nose and licking it. "Take that, ye slimy scoundrel!"

5 days

On **Tuesday**,
Captain **Beastlie**
stomped up on deck.

His socks left **pongy** patches on the nice, clean planks. "Only **4 days** left till m'birthday!" he bellowed, **rootling** a glob of peanut butter out of his ear.

4 days

"**Aharr!** There ye be, ye scurvy snack!"

On Wednesday, Captain Beastlie climbed the mast. His fingers left **filthy**, green fungus all over the **spotless** rigging. "Only **3 days** left till m'birthday," he hollered. Just then, his holey trousers let the breeze in around his bottom.

3 days

On Thursday, Captain Beastlie yelled for the ship's cook. "Only 2 days left till m'birthday!" he growled. "Where's the jam for my breakfast, Ye lily-livered limpet?"

"All over yer jacket, Cap'n Beastlie, sir!"
said the cook, saluting.
Captain Beastlie rubbed his
toast on his jacket, butter-side down.
"Nummity-num!"

2 days

On Friday, Captain Beastlie kicked his mucky, messy clothes around the cabin. "Only **1 day** left till m'birthday!" he chortled, sniffing a whiffy, rotten shirt. "Avast m'anchovies, that's luvverly!"

1 day

Late that night, there was a **rustling** and a **sneaking** all over the ship as his crew tiptoed about.

Captain Beastlie snored noisily through it all.

"SNORE! SNORE! SNORE!"

On Saturday, Captain Beastlie woke early. "Aharr! NO days to m'birthday!" he sang very loudly.

my birthday

Then he stopped and looked round his cabin.

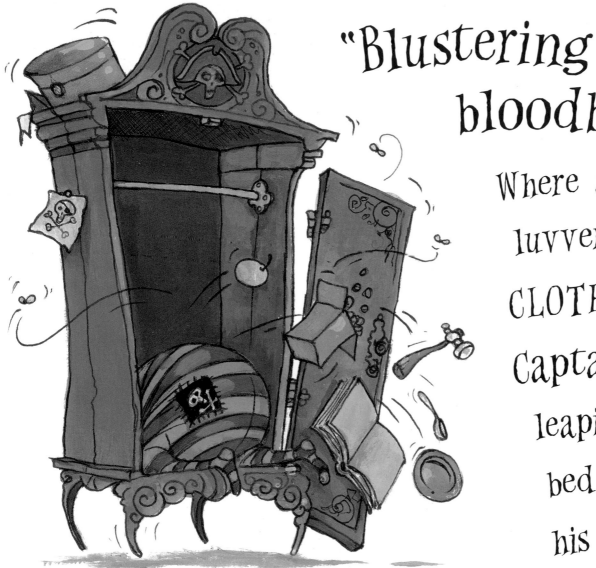

"Blustering bloodblisters! Where are all my luvverly, grubbly CLOTHES?" yelled Captain Beastlie, leaping out of bed to check his wardrobe.

Captain Beastlie stormed out of his cabin and out onto the deck . . .

"SCRUB-A-DUB-DUB! BIRTHDAY SURPRISE!" shouted his crew, as they grabbed him and popped him into a **big, bubbly** tub and gave him a **big, bubbly** scrub.

BUCCANEER'S BUBBLES

They combed out his **tangly** hair and beard . . .

. . . and wrapped him in a **clean** towel . . .

. . . then **Captain Beastlie** spotted a brightly-wrapped parcel.

Inside was . . .

... a brand new pirate suit and hat. "Happy Birthday to you! Happy Birthday to you!

Happy Birthday, dear Cap'n—
Now you don't smell of poo!"
sang his crew.

Then they all sat down to a
great, big skull cake
birthday
feast.

"Cheers, m'hearties!"

growled the

cleanest, shiniest

pirate to sail the

Seven Salty Seas . . .

. . . until he slurped
icky-sticky crumbs
all down his
brand new suit.

"Oops!"

said Captain Beastlie.